Francis
— THE LITTLE FOX —

Written by Véronique Boisjoly

Illustrated by Katty Maurey

Kids Can Press

Originally published in French under the title *Renaud le petit renard*
by Les Éditions de la Pastèque

English translation rights arranged through VéroK Agency
© 2012 Les Éditions de la Pastèque
Text © Véronique Boisjoly
Illustrations © Katty Maurey
English translation © 2013 Kids Can Press
English translation by Yvette Ghione and Karen Li

Kids Can Press acknowledges the financial support of the Government of Ontario, through the Ontario Media Development Corporation's Ontario Book Initiative; the Ontario Arts Council; the Canada Council for the Arts; and the Government of Canada, through the CBF, for our publishing activity.

Published in Canada by
Kids Can Press Ltd.
25 Dockside Drive
Toronto, ON M5A 0B5

Published in the U.S. by
Kids Can Press Ltd.
2250 Military Road
Tonawanda, NY 14150

www.kidscanpress.com

The artwork in this book was rendered digitally.
The text is set in Otari.

English edition edited by Yvette Ghione
Original edition edited by Sophie Chisogne
Designed by Stéphane Ulrich

This book is smyth sewn casebound.
Manufactured in Shenzhen, China, in 4/2013 through Asia Pacific Offset

CM 13 0 9 8 7 6 5 4 3 2 1

Library and Archives Canada Cataloguing in Publication

Boisjoly, Véronique
[Renaud le petit renard. English]
    Francis, the little fox / written by Véronique Boisjoly ; illustrated by Katty Maurey.

Translation of: Renaud le petit renard.
ISBN 978-1-894786-40-9

    I. Maurey, Katty II. Title III. Title: Renaud le petit renard. English.

PS8603.O36775R4513 2013   jC843'.6   C2013-900003-8

Kids Can Press is a *corus*™ Entertainment company

Meet Francis.

A handsome and mild-mannered fellow,
Francis is always well dressed.

Even on laundry days.

Most people wear any old thing to wash their favorite outfits, but not Francis.

Francis is new to the laundromat.

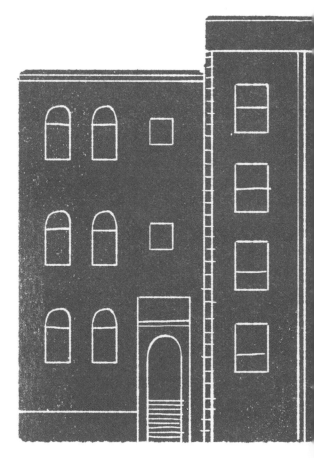

Since his father moved to an apartment, they have had to take their laundry to Mr. Li's Small Socks Laundromat.

At first, Francis didn't like the idea. It was so much easier to wash their things at home.

But bit by bit, a trip to the laundromat became
the perfect excuse to escape from his sister,
the little and too-noisy Lola.

Now Francis always looks forward to Laundry Saturdays with his father.

There are many rules at the laundromat.

No
walkie-talkies

No
trumpets

The laundromat is for behaving, not for being loud.

No tomato slingshots

NO cell phones

ABSOLUTELY **NO** pots and pans!!

Francis usually draws while his father reads the newspaper.

Saturdays are peaceful at the laundromat …

Except when Mr. Li's granddaughter, Lily Rain Boots, is there!

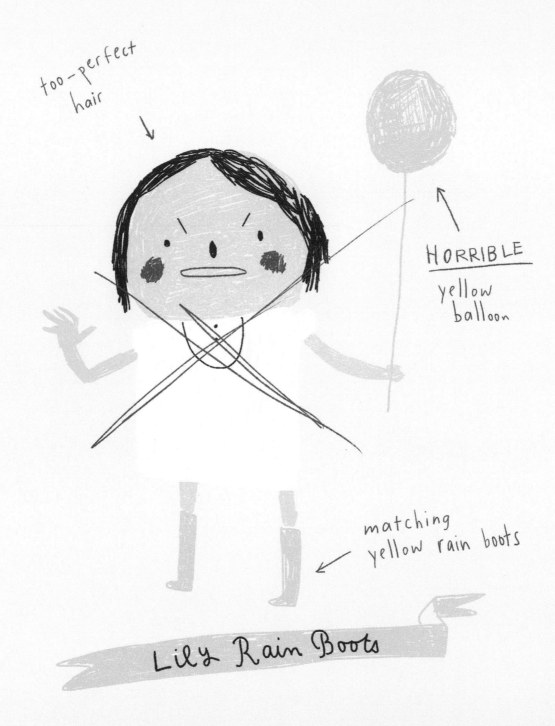

Lily Rain Boots is *trouble*. When she's bored, she likes to play tricks. And the days are long at her grandfather's laundromat.

When Francis nears the laundromat, he crosses his fingers and looks around, hoping that Lily won't be there.

Madame
Bernadette

Madame
Bernadette's
laundry basket

If she is, she's sure to play a trick on him. It happens every time!

But Lily isn't there today. Still, Francis feels only slightly relieved, because even if he doesn't *see* Lily, his fox-sense tells him that she isn't very far away ...

While they sort their laundry, Francis and his father make a list of the things that make their Laundry Saturdays so much fun.

#1

GETTING RID OF <u>DUST MITES</u>

Help!

RUN FOR YOUR LIVES!

What could be better than freshly washed clothes and bedsheets?

2

MIXING PATTERNS
AND MAKING UP STORIES

When Mr. Li isn't around, Francis and his father make a game of tossing their orphan socks onto the caribou antlers mounted above the window.

 4

EATING
frozen yogurt!

While the loads of laundry spin, the food-loving little fox enjoys a wild berry frozen yogurt at the shop down the street.

On their way back, Francis and his father sit
on a bench and slowly finish their cones while
they wait for the wash cycle to end.

Meanwhile, back at the laundromat, Lily Rain Boots pops out of her hiding spot to play a trick on Francis.

Lily grabs the laundry detergent and adds some to the Foxes' machines — *too much* detergent.

MUCH TOO MUCH!

A few seconds later (LET'S SAY 12 SECONDS), the washing machine overflows, and soon there are soap bubbles EVERYWHERE.

Lily, the little rascal, has a wonderful time!

Just as Francis and his father walk in the door, Mr. Li, curious about Lily's laughter and the racket the machines are making, comes out of his office. He sees the huge mess — and that Mouse the cat, frightened by the soapy flood, is about to make his escape!

"Mouse!" he shouts, hoping to make him stay.

Frazzled by everything happening around her, Madame Bernadette forgets the cat's name and thinks there's a *real* mouse in the laundromat.

She hops up and down on her chair, shrieking, "A mouse?! Where?!"

Francis and his father run after Mr. Li to help him catch Mouse.

Puzzled passersby look on and wonder, *Who are these silly people calling for a mouse the way you call for a cat?*

While Mr. Li and the Foxes search the neighborhood, the wash cycle ends and the rinse cycle begins.

Lily Rain Boots just can't resist ...
She's ready for even more fun!

But when she looks at the mess she's made, Lily feels
(a bit) guilty, so she picks up the mop to clean the floor.

Once she's done, Lily notices that Madame Bernadette has also joined the search for Mouse, leaving her basket of freshly folded laundry on the table.

Minutes later, Francis sees Lily leave the laundromat looking impish. He's sure she's been up to some mischief, but now's the time to look for missing cats, not to follow rascally girls.

They look around,
shout "*Mouse!*"

MOOOUUSE!

HEEERE, MOUSE!

at the top
of their lungs

and search high and low, but it's no use.

MOUSE?

There is no sign of the cat.

Where could he be hiding?

After a while, Mr. Li returns to the laundromat. Francis and Lily decide to stay outside to watch for Mouse. They look like two students being kept after school.

Neither one says a word.

Suddenly, Francis hears a faint meow —
it's coming from above!

The little fox looks up, up, up and finally spots a petrified Mouse, crouching on the roof of the laundromat.

Then Francis gets an idea — he knows just how to rescue him.

He runs into the laundromat and comes out seconds later $\left(\begin{smallmatrix}\text{LET'S SAY 56}\\ \text{SECONDS}\end{smallmatrix}\right)$ with a bedsheet, and the grown-ups following close behind. Everyone holds the sheet open and calls for Mouse to jump.

Mouse pussyfoots a little. Then he gathers his courage,
closes his eyes and lets himself fall through the air.

(WHICH IS PRETTY BRAVE
FOR A SCAREDY-CAT!)

No sooner has he landed in the sheet ...

... than the scaredy-cat leaps up and tries to escape again!

Happily, this time Mouse is not as quick as Mr. Li, who snatches him up lickety-split!

Everyone laughs. Francis and Lily are glad that this adventure has a happy ending for Mouse and Mr. Li.

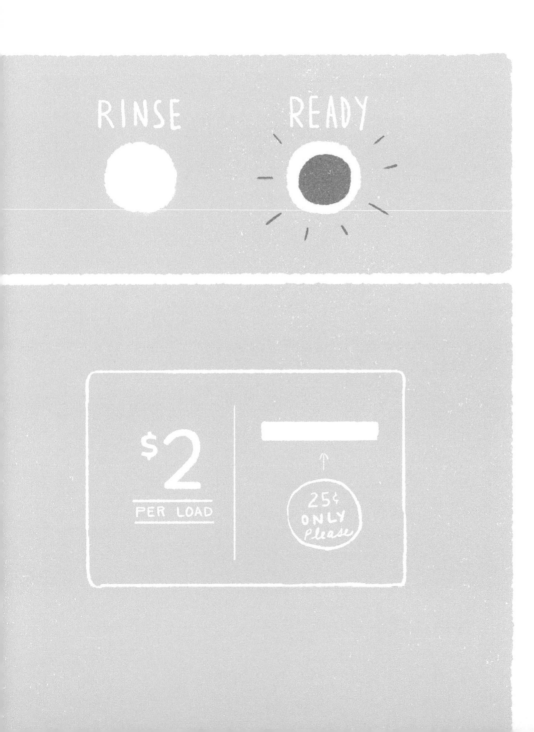

Later, at home, Francis and his father are in for one last surprise ...

At the very bottom of their laundry bag, mixed in with the still-damp clothes ...

Francis discovers ...

Madame Bernadette's

GIANT UNDERPANTS!